The Maze

Level 4A

Written by Deborah Chancellor
Illustrated by Monica Armino
Reading Consultant: Betty Franchi

About Phonics

Spoken English uses more than 40 speech sounds. Each sound is called a *phoneme*. Some phonemes relate to a single letter (d-o-g) and others to combinations of letters (sh-ar-p). When a phoneme is written down, it is called a *grapheme*. Teaching these sounds, matching them to their written form, and sounding out words for reading is the basis of phonics.

Early phonics instruction gives children the tools to sound out, blend, and say the words without having to rely on memory or guesswork. This instruction gives children the confidence and ability to read unfamiliar words, helping them progress toward independent reading.

About the Consultant

Betty Franchi is an American educator with a Bachelor's Degree in Elementary and Middle Education as well as a Master's Degree in Special Education. Betty holds a National Boards for Professional Teaching Standards certification. Throughout her 24 years as a teacher, she has studied and developed an expertise in Phonetic Awareness and has implemented phonetic strategies, teaching many young children to read, including students with special needs.

Reading tips

This book focuses on the $\bar{a}$ sound (made with the letter formation *a-e*) as in g**am**e.

Tricky and/or new words in this book

Any words in bold may have unusual spellings or are new and have not yet been introduced.

> **Tricky and/or new words in this book**
>
> **wow   want**
> **face   race**

Extra ways to have fun with this book

After the readers have finished the story, ask them questions about what they have just read.

Did you learn any new words in the book?
Which page was your favorite and why?

This way to the AMAZING maze!

A Pronunciation Guide

This grid contains the sounds used in the stories in levels 4, 5, and 6 and a guide on how to say them.

/ă/ as in pat	/ā/ as in pay	/âr/ as in care	/ä/ as in father
/b/ as in bib	/ch/ as in church	/d/ as in deed/ milled	/ĕ/ as in pet
/ē/ as in bee	/f/ as in fife/ phase/ rough	/g/ as in gag	/h/ as in hat
/hw/ as in which	/ĭ/ as in pit	/ī/ as in pie/ by	/îr/ as in pier
/j/ as in judge	/k/ as in kick/ cat/ pique	/l/ as in lid/ needle (nēd'l)	/m/ as in mom
/n/ as in no/ sudden (sŭd'n)	/ng/ as in thing	/ŏ/ as in pot	/ō/ as in toe
/ô/ as in caught/ paw/ for/ horrid/ hoarse	/oi/ as in noise	/ʊ/ as in took	/ū/ as in cute

/ou/ as in **ou**t	/p/ as in **p**op	/r/ as in **r**oar	/s/ as in **s**auce
/sh/ as in **sh**ip/ di**sh**	/t/ as in **t**igh**t**/ stopp**ed**	/th/ as in **th**in	/th/ as in **th**is
/ŭ/ as in c**u**t	/ûr/ as in **ur**ge/ t**er**m/ f**ir**m/ w**or**d/ h**ear**d	/v/ as in **v**al**v**e	/w/ as in **w**ith
/y/ as in **y**es	/z/ as in **z**ebra/ x**y**lem	/zh/ as in vi**s**ion/ plea**s**ure/ gara**g**e/	/ə/ as in **a**bout/ it**e**m/ **e**dibl**e**/ gall**o**p/ circ**u**s
/ər/ as in butt**er**			

Be careful not to add an /uh/ sound to /s/, /t/, /p/, /c/, /h/, /r/, /m/, /d/, /g/, /l/, /f/ and /b/. For example, say /fff/ not /fuh/ and /sss/ not /suh/.

Jake and Jane see a maze.
"**Wow**!" Jake says,
"I **want** to go in!"

Jane makes a **face**.
"I don't like mazes."

Jake takes a cake out of his bag.
"If you go in the maze, you can
have this cake," Jake says.

Jake runs into the maze.
He waves the cake at Jane.
"Come on!" he yells.

Jane chases Jake.

"I want cake!" she cries.

Jake and Jane get lost in the maze.
They are stuck in the maze for
a long time.

"I give up," says Jake.
Jane's tummy begins to rumble.
Jake's tummy begins to rumble too.

"Can we have the cake now?"
Jane asks.

The cake is very good.
Jane and Jane cheer up.
"Let's have a **race**!" Jake says.

Jake and Jane race
around the maze.

Will Jane find the way out?
Will Jake find it first?

"I won!" Jane shouts. "I like mazes."

OVER **48** TITLES IN SIX LEVELS
Betty Franchi recommends...

Other titles to enjoy from Level 4

Eve the Knight
978 1 84898 773 9

Fairy Fay's Bad Day
978 1 84898 772 2

Pirate School
978 1 84898 774 6

Some titles from Level 5

Snapped by Sam!
978 1 84898 775 3

Max's Trip
978 1 84898 776 0

George the Genius Gerbil
978 1 84898 777 7

Some titles from Level 6

What Wally Wanted
978 1 84898 779 1

Superhero Ed!
978 1 84898 780 7

The Robot Bop
978 1 84898 782 1

An Hachette Company
First Published in the United States by TickTock, an imprint of Octopus Publishing Group.
www.octopusbooksusa.com

Copyright © Octopus Publishing Group Ltd 2013

Distributed in the US by
Hachette Book Group USA
237 Park Avenue, New York NY 10017, USA

Distributed in Canada by
Canadian Manda Group
165 Dufferin Street, Toronto, Ontario, Canada M6K 3H6

ISBN 978 1 84898 771 5

Printed and bound in China
10 9 8 7 6 5 4 3 2 1